Guess what day it is!

SUNDAY   MONDAY   TUESDAY   WEDN

4   5   6   7

FIRST DAY
OF SCHOOL!
MUST BE
ON TIME!

11   13   14

Grandpa's
137th
Birthday   19   20 National Lettuce Day   21

26   27   28

"I canNOT
be late today!"

Racing stripes? Check!

Helmet? Check!

Stopwatch? Check!

Super Tortoise lunch box? Check!

Little Tortoise takes off—faster than
you can say LICKETY-SPLIT!

LICKETY-SPLIT again!

LICKETY-SPLIT LOUDER!

LICKETY-SPL— There she goes!

HURRY, Little Tortoise, Time for School!

Carrie Finison
Erin Kraan

RANDOM HOUSE STUDIO ■ NEW YORK

It's a good thing Little Tortoise
fueled up with extra lettuce this
morning because today she is
going to be FAST.
Faster than fast!
Faster than Super Tortoise!

Plonk-a plunk.
Plonk-a plunk.

Her feet are a blur!

Maybe she'll be the first one to school!

For the first time EVER!

Or maybe not.

Sha-shoom!

"Right behind you!"

Plonk-a plunk.
Plonk-a plunk.

Cheetah is always the first one to school.
Cheetahs are fast.

"Hurry, Little T!"

But Little Tortoise is fast, too!
As fast as a race car!
As fast as a rocket!

But not quite as fast as a llama.

"See you there, Little Tortoise!"

"Yep! See you!"

Little Tortoise hurries as fast as she can. She is probably setting a new land speed record for tortoises.

Plonk-a plunk.
Plonk-a plunk.

It doesn't matter if she won't be first, or second.

Wock-a-pa,
wock-a-pa!

Or third. Or fourth.
Or fifth. Or sixth.

"Hey, down there!"

Boing-ga,
boing-ga!

Plonk-a plunk,
plonk-a plunk.

"You're running out of time!"

"Don't be late!"

Boing-ga, boing-ga!

"Better hurry!"

"I am hurrying!" said Little Tortoise.

Little Tortoise zooms like the wind.

A slow wind.

More of a gentle breeze, really.

Sha-shoom!

"Forgot something!"

Plonk-a plunk.
Plonk-a plunk.

Maybe—*maybe*—Little Tortoise
won't be the last one to school!

Give her a minute.

This happens all the time.

I'm still hurrying!

What's all
the noise?

"Gotta roll, gotta roll,
gotta get there on time!"
Oh dear, is the WHOLE WORLD
faster than Little Tortoise?

Bumba-
da-bumba-da-bumba-da

Yes. They are.

"Want a ride?" asks Snail.
"Thanks . . . but I don't think that
would work," replies Little Tortoise.
"Okay. See you at school! Better hurry!"

Little Tortoise is left in the dust.

PTOOEY!

ka-SQUEE! ka-SQUEE!
ka-SQUEE!

"Hurry up, Little T!"

Sha-shoom!

The gust tumbles Little Tortoise
around . . . and over . . . and shell-side down.

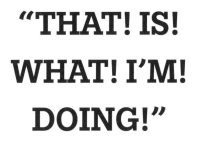

"THAT! IS!
WHAT! I'M!
DOING!"

"HELP! SOMEONE?"

No one hears.

Everyone is already inside. Having fun.

Starting school.

Without her.

Plip-plip-plop.

Her tears drop.

Little Tortoise sinks her head

deep into her shell.

But then—Little Tortoise feels herself
turning
around
and over . . .

. . . and shell-side UP!
MR. SLOTH?

"I'm running late today.
It happens to me a lot."

"Me too."

"But I'm trying to do better this
year. The important thing is,
we're here now."

Little Tortoise smiles.

She can tell that she and her teacher have a lot in common.

Little Tortoise checks her stopwatch.
They're not officially late—YET!

"HURRY, MR. SLOTH!"

"Let's do it!"

As fast as she can (which is not very fast), Little Tortoise rushes up the stairs.

NO RUNNING

SLOW DOWN!

As fast as *he* can (which is not very fast), Mr. Sloth pushes open the door. Against all the rules, they race down the hall, inch by inch.

By inch,
by inch,
by inch.
For 347 inches.

"We. Are.
Fast!"

"Yes. We.
Are!"

"And sixth!"

"Let's rock and roll!"

"Good morning, class! Sometimes we're fast, and sometimes we're last. The important thing is that we're all here."

It's the very first day, and
everyone in Mr. Sloth's class
was on time. ALMOST everyone.

**I OVERSLEPT!
WAIT FOR ME!**

Hurry, Little Hare!

Thump-ity THUMP,
Thump-ity THUMP

For Mia —C.F.

For my darling nieces, Brielle and Brooke —E.K.

Text copyright © 2022 by Carrie Finison
Jacket art and interior illustrations copyright © 2022 by Erin Kraan

All rights reserved. Published in the United States by Random House Studio, an imprint of Random House Children's Books, a division of Penguin Random House LLC, New York.

Random House Studio with colophon is a trademark of Penguin Random House LLC.

Visit us on the Web! rhcbooks.com

Educators and librarians, for a variety of teaching tools, visit us at RHTeachersLibrarians.com

Library of Congress Cataloging-in-Publication Data
Names: Finison, Carrie, author. | Kraan, Erin, illustrator.
Title: Hurry, Little Tortoise, time for school! / by Carrie Finison ; illustrated by Erin Kraan.
Description: First edition. | New York : Random House Children's Books, [2022] |
Audience: Ages 3–7. | Summary: In order to be on time for her first day of school, Little Tortoise hurries and goes as fast as she can, but despite her best efforts she is passed by all her friends along the way.
Identifiers: LCCN 2021040251 (print) | LCCN 2021040252 (ebook) | ISBN 978-0-593-30566-9 (hardcover) | ISBN 978-0-593-30567-6 (lib. bdg.) | ISBN 978-0-593-30568-3 (ebook)
Subjects: CYAC: Turtles—Fiction. | School—Fiction. | Tardiness—Fiction. | LCGFT: Picture books. Classification: LCC PZ7.1.F5358 Hu 2022 (print) | LCC PZ7.1.F5358 (ebook) | DDC [E]—dc23

MANUFACTURED IN CHINA

10 9 8 7 6 5 4 3 2 1

First Edition